The Cat in the Christmas Tree

A Magical Tail

by
Peter Scottsdale

to Halle,

Copyright

Chapter 1

He ripped around the corner and scrambled onto the sofa, running over Justen and spilling his Christmas drink.

Eggnog flew through the air. A creamy mess landed on Justen, the couch, end table, and t.v. remote control. The cat bolted across the furniture, bounding from chair to chair.

"For the love of Pete," Justen said. "My nog."

The black, green-eyed nine-month-old feline raced up the drapes and hung on by his claws. He twisted his head around until he faced the Christmas tree. The evergreen pine stood six feet high. Glass ball decorations of blue and red and green hung from its branches. Garland strung around the tree mixed with blinking white lights. On the top branch, a golden star flashed its shiny glow.

Justen wiped off the eggnog with his hands and rubbed it on his shirt.

"Sara, that cat is on thin ice. He spilt my drink and I've about had it."

His wife appeared from the kitchen, cleaning icing from

her hands with a towel. She put one hand on her hip.

"Shadow, be good. Where is he?" she said and looked about the room.

"Up the curtain again."

"Oh, you bad cat. I'll get him."

Sara moved to the front window, tucking the towel into her red and green apron.

"We've got to do something about him. I swear if he causes more trouble, I will-" Justen said.

"He's young. He's still learning. What were you like as a kid?" she said and reached out to take hold of Shadow.

"You can say that about Nathan — and this isn't about me. This is about this cat. He's a mischief maker, that's for sure," Justen said.

Sara touched the cat's black fur and he hurtled himself onto the Christmas tree. The evergreen toppled over. Ornament balls came loose and smashed to the hardwood floor. Lights twisted on the branches. The glittering star crashed into many pieces and Shadow sprinted out of the fallen pine, wrapped in garland. With a string of silver dragging behind him, he tore out of the living room and down the hall toward the bedrooms.

"Oh no! We worked on that tree all last night," Sara said.

"Rascal! That cat's life in this house is on a short leash," Justen said.

Sara's husband got to his feet and rushed to the tree. He bent down and took hold of the tree trunk. Lifting it up, he slid it back into the tree stand. More ornaments bashed to the floor. Several branches were broken and the lights hung to one side of the evergreen.

"Careful," Sara said.

"I am being careful," her husband said.

Eight-year-old Nathan walked into the living room. His eyes drew wide and his jaw dropped. He gasped.

"What was that noise? What happened to the Christmas tree?" Nathan asked.

"Your cat is what happened. If Shadow doesn't smarten up, he's gone – out of this house," Justen said, pointing his thumb over his shoulder.

"No, Dad."

"Justen, don't say that," Sara said.

"No! I'm tired of this cat and his antics. He scratches the furniture, wakes us up when he wants to be fed at five in the morning. He pushed your grandmother's antique snow globe off the shelf, breaking it wide open. That was intentional. I saw him do it. Not an accident. Not only that, he's knocked other stuff off the counter, smashing tea cups, plates and bowls. He ripped apart the screen on every window and both doors. And he fell through the basement ceiling, bringing down some tiles. We still don't know how he got up there. Now he knocked over the Christmas tree, making a mess of all the work we put in decorating it. He's a rotten cat. One more thing and that cat is gone," Justen said. His arms flailed, his face red.

"No, Daddy. Please. He'll be good. You'll see." Tears dripped out of Nathan's eyes. He clasped his hands together and shook them.

"Yes, Nathan."

"Mommy?"

"We'll discuss this later. It's Christmas Eve. Let's clean this mess up. Santa's coming," Nathan's mom said.

Nathan wiped his tears on his ugly Christmas reindeer sweater sleeve and smiled. "I'll help," he said.

"Okay, but be careful. There's some sharp glass. You could cut yourself."

"Okay, Mom. I'll get the broom."

Sara picked up the glass ball pieces and Nathan swept up the remaining mess. Justen straightened the remaining decorations. Their son emptied the dustpan into the kitchen garbage bin and disappeared down the hall. Mom returned to the kitchen and Nathan came back to the tree.

"Look what I got," he said, holding up the silver garland.

"Let's put it back on the tree," Dad said.

Soon, they stood back and looked at the scene before them.

"How does it look, my son?" Justen asked.

"Wonderful."

"If you say so."

"I do," Nathan said.

"Get washed up for supper," Sara called from the kitchen.

Nathan and his dad washed up in the bathroom. But before going to the kitchen table with his parents, Nathan stopped by the Christmas tree. Alone by the pine, he peered upward at it and held his hands together. He drew in a deep breath.

"Mr. Christmas Tree, I'm sorry Shadow hurt you. Daddy's gonna make me give him away, but I love him. I will miss my kitty if he's gone. So please, Mr. Christmas Tree, help us. Don't let Shadow jump on you again. I don't know how to stop him so please stop him. I love Shadow. Okay?" Nathan said.

The boy touched a branch and rubbed some needles between

his fingers. He smiled with a sigh.

"Thank you," Nathan said.

"Nathan, come for supper. We're having your favorite," his mother said.

"Yum," he said. "I gotta go." He let go of the branch and ran to the kitchen.

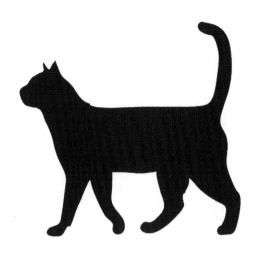

Chapter 2

After pork chops, mashed potatoes and carrots, the Branson family nestled into the sofa and turned on *How the*

Grinch Stole Christmas. A commercial rolled after the Grinch stole the Christmas gifts and decorations.

"The Grinch is a bad…bad…thing. What is a Grinch?" Nathan asked, scratching his cheek.

"He's green and hairy," Mom said, patting her son's hand.

"Like Shadow. Only he's black and hairy," the boy said.

"Shadow's bad too. He might end up in Whoville with the Who people," Dad said.

"Can I go too?" Nathan said, smiling.

"No."

"Aww."

"Justen, not now."

Dad shook off his wife and son and went to the fridge. He popped open a Pepsi and headed downstairs to his man cave. A few moments later, the sound video game shooting and explosions was carried upstairs.

Nathan faced his mother, his eyes wide. "Do we have to

give Shadow away if he knocks down the Christmas tree again?" he asked.

"We'll see, honey."

"No, Mommy. I don't want him to go. He's a good kitty." Nathan rubbed her arm and nodded. She took his hands in hers.

"Nathan, Shadow is a naughty kitty and keeps wrecking things. He's out of control. He wakes us up to be fed or petted. We need our sleep, especially Daddy. He works long hours at the construction site. He does dangerous work and cannot be tired all the time. It's very dangerous. He could get hurt or he could hurt someone else. Do you want that?"

"No," Nathan said and pushed and twisted his index fingers together. "Why don't you keep your door closed at night? Maybe that will work."

"Then I can't hear you."

"Why do you need to hear me?"

"To keep you safe. To make sure you're okay in your bedroom," Mommy said, tapping his nose.

"I'm okay, Mommy. So is Shadow. You don't need to worry about us. He's a good kitty. He won't crash the Christmas tree again. I promise."

"How can you promise that?" she asked.

"I asked the Christmas tree to keep Shadow from knocking it over."

"And how's it going to stop him?"

Nathan's eyebrows arched, his finger went to his temple and tapped his head. He shrugged. His eyes widened and his mouth opened into a smile.

"Because he's a magical Christmas tree," Nathan said.

"To be a kid again," she said. Pulling her son close, she laughed. Running her fingers through his hair, she said, "I wish that were true."

"Oh, it is. You'll see." He pointed at her.

Shadow came into the room and headed to the Christmas tree. He raised his head and sniffed the lower branches. One paw batted some pine needles that bobbed up and down on the branch.

"No, Shadow," Sara said, dragging the "o" sound out and long.

The dark cat turned and leapt onto the couch. He eased his paws onto Nathan's lap and bonked his head into the little boy's face. Nathan kissed him.

"See, he's a good cat," Nathan said and hugged Shadow. Sara scratched the feline around his ears.

"He is beautiful, that's for sure. I love cats," she said.

The cat purred and pushed into the boy again. Followed by some light claw kneading into Nathan's round tummy.

"It's 9:00 o'clock. Time for little boys to go to bed," Mommy said.

"Aww, can't I stay up late tonight? It's Christmas Eve."

His mother shook her head and tapped her watch.

"Santa's coming. And he wants all good children to get a good night's sleep before opening their presents in the morning. You want to keep Santa happy, don't you?" Mom said.

Her son nodded and said, "Un, uh."

She hugged him tight, rubbing her hands up and down his back.

"Besides, Santa will come faster the earlier you go to sleep," Sara said.

"Yay!" He clapped his hands together once. "Can Shadow sleep with me again?"

"Yes, he can. Time for bed."

"Goody."

Sara held onto Nathan and stood up, carrying her son to his bedroom. He touched the silver star decorations hanging from the ceiling that had been out of reach before. Shadow followed them.

Once in his bedroom, Mommy helped him get his pajamas on and tucked him in. His cat jumped onto the bed and cuddled into the crook of his knees. Nathan's mother turned out the light after a kiss on Nathan's forehead and a kiss on Shadow's whiskers.

She left the door ajar. Enough room so Shadow could

leave to use the litter box if he needed to. Nathan drifted away into slumber land with a purring pussycat by his side. Shadow slept until his night instincts kicked in.

His head popped up. Looking around, Shadow got up and sniffed Nathan's face, his whiskers twitching and tickling the boy's cheek. Half awake, Nathan brushed the cat's face away. Shadow left Nathan and dropped down to the carpet. He squeezed through the doorway and headed down the hall toward the living room and the Christmas tree.

After all, the night was still young for a naughty kitty.

Chapter 3

Nathan's parents sat on the floor surrounded by Christmas wrap, tape, ribbons and scissors. Justen wrapped a

Tonka truck and Sara a hockey stick.

"This isn't as easy to wrap as you might think," Sara said. "The paper keeps sliding off."

"You need some help?" Justen asked.

"I got it."

She taped and twisted the wrapping paper around the shaft. They finished wrapping the gifts and sat back admiring their work.

"The tree looks pretty good – considering," Sara said.

"Sure does."

Shadow raced into the living room and ripped up the green tree, knocking off some of the remaining ornaments. He stopped three quarters of the way up and peered through the needles. His claws gripped the branch. Tilting his head, he meowed.

"That darn cat. I swear he's going back to the SPCA," Justen said.

"That would break Nathan's heart, Justen."

"Sara, something has to be done. This can't keep happening. I'm tired of it."

"We'll figure something out. I heard a cat whisperer might be able to help. We could try that."

"And how much would that cost?" Justen said.

"I don't know. Shadow's so bad, but there's no obedience school for cats."

Sara got up and went to the tree. She reached into the branches and took hold of the

mischievous puss. Shadow sunk
his sharp teeth into her wrist,
drawing blood.

"Oww."

Sara let go and snapped her
hand back. Justen inspected the
wound. He retrieved some tissue
from the end table and pressed
it on the bite mark.

Justen looked his wife in
the eye. She revealed the wound
to her husband. The bleeding
stopped.

"It's only a small hole,"
Sara said.

"What if that was Nathan?" Justen asked.

Sara sighed. "Okay, you've made your point. But after the holidays. I don't want Nathan remembering he lost his cat at Christmas time."

"All right. In the new year that cat'll be long gone," Justen said.

"Do you think the tree will survive until tomorrow?" Sara asked and smiled.

"That's a question for the ages."

Shadow pounced out of the tree and tackled a mouse toy stuffed with catnip. He lurched to one side and dropped to the floor, kicking the fake rodent with his hind feet. Then he ran out of the room with his feet sliding on the hardwood floor trying to get traction. Nathan's parents laughed.

"It's hard to get rid of a cat that is so funny, even though he's bad," Sara said.

"I know, but he's got to go," Justen said.

"Yeah, I know. After the holidays, Shadow will be up for adoption at the SPCA. Even though I don't like it, it has to be done. C'mon, it's time for bed. Santa's coming."

Sara giggled and took her husband's hand. They shut off the lights and went to bed, leaving the black cat in the dark.

Chapter 4

Shadow followed them to the bedroom, but Justen shoved him out. The dark feline turned and crossed the hall into Nathan's room. He leapt onto the bed and walked on the boy up his face. Shadow pushed a front foot into Nathan's jaw and meowed.

Nathan woke up and petted his cat until he fell back asleep. The kitty tried again to wake him but failed. He plopped down to the floor. Leaving the bedroom, Shadow trotted down the hall.

He came back to the catnip mouse and smacked it about — zigzagging throughout the home.

The feline stopped and with a wild-eyed look on his face, darted out of the dining room and down the corridor. He dug his claws into the carpet for grip and ran back and forth. Each time it thundered like a herd of water buffalo.

"Rotten cat," Justen said and fell back to sleep.

Shadow stopped and sat in the kitchen. He smelled his food dish and ate the remaining morsels from his supper. His rough tongue licked his chops and cleaned his front paws and face.

Afterwards, he gazed at the hanging decorations and sprung into the air to capture one. But his leaping fell short. He dropped down without his prize. He tried again but missed. No silver star for Shadow this Christmas Eve. The cat let out a long, loud yowl.

"Shadow, shut up. We're trying to sleep," came Dad's weary voice.

The black cat turned and walked toward the evergreen. Batting some needles, he moved beneath the Christmas pine. The branches up and down the trunk quivered.

Shadow investigated, looking and smelling and touching it with his whiskers. He stretched out his legs, arching his back. His claws protruded. Something touched his back.

The dark feline pivoted and found only the tree and the

gifts beneath it. His back twitched. One ear twisted and lay flat. His eyes narrowed. The cat turned and stepped away.

Going into the dining room, he sat under the table and stared at the Christmas tree. It shook slightly. Shadow sprinted back into the living room, sending the mat flying behind him. He ran to the pine, threw himself into the air and nose-dived into its branches.

Then Shadow disappeared.

Chapter 5

Shadow landed on all fours in two-inch snow. His warm breath billowed out of his nostrils into the cold night air. The stars and moon shone their light onto the scene below.

"What the fur? What's happening? Where am I? Am I talking like a human? What's going on?" Shadow said, searching the darkness.

"You're in the Great Wondrous Woods."

Shadow leapt three feet straight up and landed back in the snow. The fur on his back and tail fluffed out.

"Who said that?" he asked. His eyes darted back and forth.

"I did. Your Christmas tree."

"No, really. Who said that?"

"Look around you. What do you see?"

Shadow viewed the area.

"Trees. Nothing but trees," Shadow said.

A branch from the nearest tree touched Shadow's shoulder, causing him to start. He spun around. A pine tree stood next to him.

"I am Mast. I am the Christmas tree you keep damaging. We're all Christmas trees here with a few exceptions."

"How did I get here?" Shadow asked.

"I brought you here. When you jumped into me, you went through my branches and into this wonderful land of Christmas trees," Mast said.

"Ooo-kay. Why am I here?"

"You've been misbehaving and will lose your home if you don't stop."

"They won't get rid of me. I'm too cute. Besides, Nathan loves me too much to lose me. I'm safe in that house."

"Are you? Come with me," the tree said.

A road opened up before them covered in snow and lined with trees.

"How is this possible?" Shadow asked.

"The magic of Christmas makes it possible."

Mast ripped his roots out of the soil. They rippled across the ground, propelling him forward. Shadow walked down the road beside him. A clearing opened in the dim woods as they approached the Village of the Living Tree — a Christmas tree town.

Lights lit the night streets in blue and white and red. Garland of gold lay from pole to pole and home to home.

Green trees moved to and fro. Reindeer grazed on grass that rose out of the snow. Strung popcorn and tinsel decorated the town.

"This is amazing. There's so much to play with here," Shadow said. He crouched and wiggled his bum, pointing at a passing pine.

"Don't do it," Mast said and blocked the cat with his branches. "This is what is getting you into trouble at home."

Shadow stood up. "But I'm still young and I love to play," he said.

Mast shook and stretched.

"Let me show you the Barker family. Over here," Mast said.

They approached a white home with emerald needles on the ground surrounding the house. Bare hooks hung on the walls. The green tree and black cat peered in the frosted window. The room was lit with string lights missing half the bulbs. A dark habitat.

"Why are they missing ornaments and bulbs?" Shadow asked.

"First let me say, each family of trees strives to be the best Christmas trees they can be for each human family. It is a matter of pride to do good work and bring joy to children and adults. We Christmas trees want every holiday to be the best. But that didn't happen here. See the small tree by the dry, brown wreath?" Mast said.

"Yes."

"He is a young one. Three days before Christmas, he was alone at home and decided to have some fun. Instead of playing with his toys, he wrapped himself in this year's ornaments and lights and danced throughout the house. He jumped on the furniture, soil mounds and beds. He ran around with decorations flying off him. The child tree also laid down on the mounds and rolled back and forth. He broke all the glass balls and burst half of the light bulbs. Now, the Barkers won't be chosen to be Christmas trees in human homes."

"I don't understand. Don't people pick out a Christmas tree and decorate it themselves?" Shadow asked.

"Yes. But as Christmas trees, we offer up the best. When our farmer, Chris, comes to pick out trees to sell to mothers and fathers, we present him with only the top rated candidates. All of us compete to be beautiful Christmas trees. It's our life's mission. The Barkers are now not able to decorate themselves and therefore were not chosen to be Christmas trees. It's a shame, really," Mast said.

"So the young Barker tree shouldn't have played with the decorations," the black cat said.

"Correct. Not everything is a play toy. Damaging things hurts those who own them. Understand?"

"I think so. I've hurt my family by playing with and breaking their stuff," Shadow said.

"Like the Christmas tree?" Mast said.

"Yes, like the Christmas tree."

"Good. Now, I've got something else to show you."

Chapter 6

"Follow me," the Christmas tree said with a point from his branches.

Mast and Shadow moved away from the Barker home and down

the street. A small tree came to them. They stopped. The little one extended his branches out to the feline, and Shadow turned to Mast.

"He's a young sapling. He's never seen a cat before," Mast said.

"That's a cat?" the infant tree said. "Cats hurt trees. They claw our branches and knock us over. My mom told me."

Mast leaned over and said, "Some even pee on us."

"Oh no. I gotta go. Mommy."
The young tree said and left in
a hurry, shuffling as fast
through the soil as his roots
would carry him.

"Do cats scare trees?"
Shadow asked.

"Yes, most do. We worry
about what you do to us."

"I had no idea we were
hurtful. I was only playing,"
the cat said.

"Sometimes playing hurts
others. And someone can even
harm themselves. You have to be

careful when you play," the tree said.

"I will from now on." He nodded.

"Also when you think you're playing, you can not only hurt someone's physical body but their feelings too. Hitting or teasing — even when you think you're playing — can make others feel bad. You don't like it when others hurt you, do you?"

"No," Shadow said, hanging his head.

"So don't do it, especially to Christmas trees. We're a sensitive bunch," Mast said.

Shadow let out a meow that ended with a purr.

"I have one more thing to show you," the evergreen said.

Chapter 7

Mast shambled toward six
small trees playing in the
distance and Shadow followed.
After growing close, they
stopped.

"Get into my branches," he said to the kitty. "I don't want you frightening the saplings."

Shadow dipped beneath Mast's lower branches and climbed up his trunk until Mast stopped him.

"Can you see the tree children?" the Christmas tree asked.

"Yes."

"Watch the tall one. His name is Forrest."

The tall tree Forrest stood over the others. He stooped down and yanked the roots of another child tree out of the soil. The sapling screamed and said, "Stop," before he fell forward.

He landed on the snowy ground and pushed his branches to get up but failed. The other young trees took his branches and righted him back up.

"Why did you do that? It hurts to push a tree over. You hurt me," he said.

"Just playing," Forrest said and laughed. He jerked toward the young tree who startled back and planted his roots back in the ground.

"Why does he do that?" Shadow asked Mast. "He's a mean tree."

"No, he's not," Mast said.

"What? Why do you say that?"

"Like most trees, cats and people, they will do what they can get away with. Just the nature of things."

"What can we do to stop it?" Shadow said.

"We tell. We speak up. We tell whoever is misbehaving to stop or be punished. It's important we tell someone in authority if someone is hurting another. I'll talk to his parents. They'll take care of him. They're good trees," Mast said.

Mast shuffled to the child trees and extended out his branches.

"Forrest, that wasn't nice. Do not knock other trees over. Now, apologize to that tree," Mast said.

Forrest stared at Mast for some time and turned to the sapling.

"I'm sorry," Forrest said.

"And...?"

"I won't do it again."

"Good tree. Now, go and play and grow," Mast said and rambled away with Shadow hidden away in his branches.

"As a society, we cannot allow anyone to be bad to others – kids or adults. That includes saying hurting, saying nasty things that hurt feelings or are untrue. Or damaging someone else's property," the Christmas tree said.

"Like a cat playing with and breaking things that I should not be playing with," Shadow said.

"And...?"

"Scratching and biting, climbing curtains, waking Mom

and Dad early in the morning for breakfast and knocking over Christmas trees."

"Yes. It hurts when you topple us," Mast said.

"Sorry, Mast. I won't do it again."

"I'm over it now. You should know Justen wanted to kick you out of his house if you kept getting into trouble. That would've broken Nathan's heart. He's such a sweet boy."

"He sure is. Thank you, Christmas tree, for showing me

how to be a good cat.
Hopefully, I won't be taken to
the animal shelter."

"I think you'll be okay,
Shadow. Now jump down and take
a run at me."

"What?"

"One last time. It's all
right."

Shadow dropped out of his
branches and ran until he got
himself a good running distance
away from Mast. He turned and
raced to the Christmas tree and

leapt into his branches and disappeared.

Chapter 8

In the dim lit living room,
Shadow appeared out of the
Christmas tree. He sailed
through the air as if he had
jumped through the tree and

landed on the other side. The cat hit the floor with all four feet. Shadow meowed, unable to talk like a human anymore. He turned around. The tree shook and was still.

"Meow," Shadow said.

He purred and walked under the tree's branches. The black cat sat among the wrapped gifts and stayed there until morning, keeping a purr in his throat.

At 6:30am, Sara came into the living room with Nathan and Justen. The boy gasped.

"Look at all the presents. Are they all for me?" Nathan said.

"Some are," Justen said.

"Can we open them?"

"Look. Shadow's under the tree. Can you hear him purring?" Sara said.

"I can. He's loud," Nathan said.

"Hey, the tree is still standing. And he didn't rip apart any gifts," Justen said.

Nathan ran to Shadow, avoiding the presents and hugged his feline.

"He's my Christmas gift," the boy said.

Shadow head bonked the kid and rubbed his fur on Nathan's face.

"See, Daddy. He's a good kitty."

"We'll see if he stays that way. Then maybe he won't have to go back to the SPCA," Justen said.

"Yay."

"Let's open some gifts. Youngest first," Sara said.

"That's Shadow," Nathan said.

The young child found a gift for the Christmas cat. He unwrapped the Kitty Kick Stix, a long, stuffed, catnip toy that Shadow pounced and held onto while he kicked it with his hind feet.

"Now, that's something he can wreck it he wants to," Dad said.

From that Christmas on,
Shadow kept the lessons he
learned from Mast, the Magical
Christmas Tree, in mind
whenever he played. Mom and Dad
let their son keep his cat.

The black kitty played and
treated all members of the
family with purrs, love and
respect the rest of his happy,
playful life.

Read All About Cats

With These Books

by Peter Scottsdale

How Do Cats Do That?

Discover How Cat Do The

Amazing Things They Do

The Wonder Of Cats

With Hundreds Of

Fascinating Facts Waiting

Inside To Be Discovered

About the Author

A cat lover from an early age, Peter Scottsdale wrote his first cat tale, "The Cat and the Dog," in a grade three creative writing exercise — the story of a cat and a dog lost in the woods, and the police shooting the dog for some reason. Peter drew inspiration for the story from Disney's *The Incredible Journey*.

Throughout his life, cats have been a welcome and influencing presence. From Tia (a Siamese) to Booties (a Tabby with White) to Rusty (an orange boy with little ears) to Sam the Siamese, Peter has loved all his felines (and still does). He's loved all his cats so much so he started to write about them. They have inspired and delighted him to create cat stories and to find feline facts for his books.

Currently, he resides in Medicine Hat, Alberta, Canada with his three cats: Tanzy (the feisty feline), Alley (the mischief maker) and Tigger (the gentle giant).

90170756R00049

Made in the USA
San Bernardino, CA
15 October 2018